The River King

Lane Walker

The Fishing Chronicles
www.lanewalkerbooks.com

ISBN 978-1-7362679-0-5
For Worldwide Distribution
Printed in the U.S.A.

The Fishing Chronicles and Hometown Hunters books
www.lanewalker.com

Special thank you to all
who have served and continue
to serve in the military
to protect our rights
and our country.
You are true heroes!

Hometown Hunters Collection

The Legend of the Ghost Buck
The Hunt for Scarface
Terror on Deadwood Lake
The Boss on Redemption Road
The Day it Rained Ducks
The Lost Deer Camp

The Fishing Chronicles

Monster of Farallon Islands
The River King
The Ice Queen

To purchase books, check out
www.lanewalker.com

~ 1 ~

"This is boring," said eight-year-old Hugh, talking to his grandpa sitting next to him on an old folding chair. The pair loved to fish together but without much success that day.

"Just keep that line in the water. Try one more cast," replied Grandpa with a smile.

The pair had been fishing from the bank of the nearby river. It was early March, and the water was still cold. Fish had just started making their way up stream, but the bites were slow. Grandpa had hoped to catch enough fish to fill his homemade smoker made from an old refrigerator.

Hugh took his pole and continued to cast his line for another fifteen minutes.

"Grandpa, let's just go home. It's too cold and the fishing aren't biting," complained Hugh.

"Keep at it, buddy, try just one more cast."

"Grandpa, I've cast at least thirty times since the last time you said that," complained Hugh.

One of his grandfather's most effective strategies for teaching his family the art of fishing was to stay positive and act as though they were one cast away from catching something.

"That's why they call it fishing—sometimes it just takes one more cast. One bite can change everything," Grandpa reminded him. "It's the idea that you could catch a wall hanger or a record book fish on your very next cast. That's what makes fishing so great."

Hugh squirmed in his cheap, plastic chair. He loved fishing with his grandpa; in fact, he loved spending time with him no matter what they did.

"Grandpa, I just think we should go. Nothing is biting and it's windy. I would stay all day if we were catching something, but we aren't. It seems like we're just wasting our time," said Hugh.

"Wasting our time? Hugh, you can learn a lot about life by casting your line in the water. It seems like today, you kids want instant everything, but that isn't how life works. Just because something isn't working out, doesn't mean you just up and quit. You could be missing out on something special," said Grandpa.

Without saying another word, Hugh pulled back his pole and cast back into the river. Ten minutes later, he felt a strong pull on the end of his line and set the hook, pulling in a big catfish.

Grandpa just smiled.

"Okay, I kind of get it, Grandpa, but it's just one fish. We've been out here a long time. I've made at least fifty more casts since the last time you said, 'one more cast,'" Hugh reminded him.

Grandpa sat upright in his chair with a sudden burst of energy.

"Hugh! I think it's time I told you a story, a special story about a once-in-a-lifetime adventure that changed my life forever. I learned a lot of things on this particular fishing adventure. One of the things I learned was that anything can happen when your line is in the water."

When Grandpa settled in to share this life-changing event, something strange, almost magical, happened. Hugh had heard hundreds of his grandpa's stories over the years because the old man was a great storyteller. His tales were exciting and always captivated his audience. Most of them revolved around hunting or fishing; some were about his days in the Navy.

When he started telling Hugh this story, however, a strange transformation took place.

Grandpa flashed back over 50 years to a simpler time when he was young, 15-year-old Bobby, chasing River Kings, and began to share his story...

~ 2 ~

It was the fall of my freshman year of high school. My three best friends and I had made plans to fish and camp down the local Cass River for three days. All of us boys grew up on the river that ran right through our hometown. River life was a normal, everyday thing for most kids at that time.

The fishing trip was supposed to be a vacation of sorts for the four of us. It was late October, and we had two extra days off of school, giving us a four-day weekend.

We began by making preparations to build a floatable raft for the trip. The raft's main purpose was to provide a place to fish from during the day and sleep on at night.

Our crew was close. We had been the best of friends since the first grade. All of us competed and played sports together; in fact, we did almost everything together.

The four of us were similar but also had different characteristics that made each of us unique.

I guess I was the ringleader of the group, probably because I was the most outspoken and wasn't afraid to make decisions. I wasn't very big back then, but I was tough.

Johnny was tall, the purest athlete of the group. He was an African-American, and he was always the best at everything he did. It didn't matter if it was basketball or playing jacks, he always was on the winning team. His determination and attitude made things interesting for the group. We all knew in advance that Johnny planned to catch the biggest fish on our trip. There wasn't even a debate about it because we all knew that Johnny would win.

David was also athletic and strong. He didn't look like a typical freshman boy. His sport was football, and he was a wrecking ball on the field. Whether playing running back or linebacker,

David always was sure to make a play. While he liked football, his true love was the outdoors. He was obsessed with hunting and fishing; he was a true outdoorsman. It was his idea for the four of us to take an adventure down the Cass River that fall.

Chris was the quietest one of the group. While he wasn't the most outgoing, when he spoke, everybody listened. He was a real tough guy; everyone around town knew not to make Chris mad. His loyalty was unmatched, and none of us ever worried about bullies when we were around Chris. We knew no matter what, Chris would take care of it.

We all stuck together and loved adventure.

It was the last Friday before a planned fall break. Teachers had professional development day, so we had the following Thursday and Friday off from school. Next Friday was Halloween.

We were all sitting in our sixth-hour science class when our teacher, Mr. Hill, began talking about fish native to the Cass River.

Mr. Hill was using a film projector to show

various pictures of the river and the species of fish in it on the white wall in our science lab.

"Now, this is the king of the river, the northern pike," said Mr. Hill.

Even though science was one of my favorite subjects, I started to get bored with the old pictures and projector.

But when the picture of the pike was displayed, that all changed. The entire class let out a gasp at the sight of the monster fish. I turned behind me and looked at David. I knew he would love seeing such a massive fish.

The picture showed Mr. Hill holding a huge pike—it had to be at least 40 inches long. The fish had a large head and prehistoric looking, razor-sharp teeth. Even though the picture wasn't in color, the fish was mesmerizing. It looked like a villain out of a comic book.

David leaned up and whispered in my ear, "Bobby, I have an idea. I think I know the perfect way to celebrate Halloween this year—a fishing trip down the river!"

~ 3 ~

The bell rang, and everyone hurried down the hallway for lunch. The lunchroom was full of excitement. At first, I thought they were all charged up about the fish picture in Mr. Hill's room.

I had forgotten that it was Friday. Every Friday, the school lunch ladies made giant chocolate chip cookies that they sold for ten cents, which accounted for the buzz in the room. Plus, we only had three days of school left next week before our four-day fall vacation, which added to the powder keg of enthusiasm.

We sat down at the back of the lunchroom at our usual table that faced the school's main parking lot.

"Guys, I have the perfect idea for a Halloween adventure," David began.

Every so often, the four of us tried to do a special activity or build something together. Last July, we spent weeks building and firing off wooden model rockets. It was a lot of fun, but one of Johnny's rockets started a fire in Mr. Williams' hay field, ending our summer recreation.

"This time let's do something totally crazy. Let's camp, fish, and float down the Cass River," David said.

"I can't swim," Chris quickly whispered, trying not to be heard and seem like a wimp.

"Don't worry, the river isn't that deep," David reassured him. "It's cold anyway, and I don't plan on getting wet. There are only a couple spots that will even be over our head."

We all loved the outdoors. Hunting and fishing were passions we shared. The idea of spending three nights on the river with my best friends with no adults bossing us around and telling us what to do sounded like a perfect plan.

"I'm down for it," said Johnny.

"In," I quickly replied.

"Sure, why not," said Chris.

That night after practice, we all met at David's house to start working out the plan for our fall adventure.

"The first thing we need to decide is when we are going," I said.

"Next Thursday, the first day of fall vacation has to be the day!" David quickly replied.

We all nodded in approval.

"Okay! The next thing is, we need to figure out how we're going to get down the river," I added.

The four of us sat in silence until Chris spoke up. "What about a giant raft, like one that Huck Finn would have built?"

"A raft would be perfect!" Johnny chimed in.

"But does anyone know how to build one?" I asked them.

"My dad can help," replied David. His dad owned a construction company that built all kinds of stuff, mostly pole barns and houses.

"Okay, so how far down the river are we going to go? Where can we put the raft in the river and where will we get it out?" asked Chris, who always was the practical one.

"I was thinking we put in behind my house," David replied, "and plan on getting it out downtown at the park. There's a dock there, so it'll be perfect. That's like a 12-mile trip!"

"Isn't that a long way to go on a raft?" Johnny questioned.

"Exactly!" David shot back. "We don't want no wimpy trip. Plus, the park is really the only place we can get the raft back out of the water."

At first, the trip sounded crazy. The idea of going down the river in itself wasn't that scary. But the route had us traveling on it for over 12 miles.

"Guys, doesn't that section of the river go by the Lost Cemetery?" Bobby asked, almost in a whisper.

"Yeah, it does, but we'll just plan on doing it during daylight, so it won't be that spooky," David explained.

The Lost Cemetery was part of our town's folklore. While the cemetery was built in the early 1800s, it had been abandoned for over 50 years. Most of the tombstones had deteriorated or been destroyed. The ones that remained were cracked and damaged from years of weathering. We had learned about the cemetery in our history class in sixth grade. The teacher took the class there every spring to explain the history of it. Some famous Civil War soldier was buried there.

The cemetery itself is spooky, but what makes it even more eerie is the fact that it is located at the end of a dead-end road, three miles from anyone or anything.

The isolated location of the cemetery added even more to the mystery of the Lost Cemetery.

~ 4 ~

We met over at David's house Sunday night to finish planning and start building our raft. I was the last one to arrive.

I noticed a bunch of lumber already out and four large, plastic barrels propped up against the pole barn. It was obvious that David's dad, Jim, had worked hard on the framing of the raft, which was perfectly square and complete. The raft looked impressive, and the frame was a perfect 12x12 square of treated lumber.

"All we have to do is put these boards across the frame and make the deck. Dad said he'd attach the barrels because it's kind of complicated," David explained.

"What do you think, Bobby?" asked Johnny with his arms folded in front of him.

"I think it looks cool," I said.

Chris looked up and smiled.

"I'm going to borrow my Uncle Eddie's pop-up tent," Johnny said with a smile. "It's an eight-by-eight tent and will fit perfect on the raft. We'll have a couple feet on each side so we can fish. It should leave us a little room to walk around."

We spent the next two hours putting down the boards and screwing them into the wooden frame. By the time we were done, we had a nice size deck. The top of our raft was complete.

The four barrels were discolored and mismatched but looked to be in decent shape. David told us his dad planned on mounting the barrels sometime during the week. He wanted to make sure they were secured to the raft correctly.

David's house, a rustic log cabin, sat on 40-acres of gorgeous land. It was the perfect location to build our raft. The back of his property connected directly to the Cass River and had a nice-sized sandy beach to launch the raft.

"I sure hope it floats," Chris said with a sigh.

"You're just saying that because you can't swim," Johnny jabbed at him.

Chris shot him a quick glare and then nodded.

"It will float, trust me," David's dad Jim said, intervening between the two boys' trash talk. He walked up behind us, and his body language told me he was impressed with the work we had done on the raft. I was somewhat nervous because we all knew, like most builders, Jim was a perfectionist.

"All the rain we got last week will help you boys. The river should be high, and you shouldn't have to worry about rocks or shallow water. There isn't a spot between here and Memorial Bridge where you shouldn't have deep enough water."

This trip wouldn't have been possible in the summer. The heat and evaporation of the hot weather lower the river, making it too shallow. The rain and high waters of the fall made the timing perfect.

The four of us were pretty confident after getting Jim's approval. I knew it meant a lot to David that his dad was proud of our work.

Everything was going great until Jim spoke up with his concerns. "It won't be the water you boys have to worry about," he said with a frown.

The four of us looked at each other, suddenly uneasy. At first, it caught me off guard. What was he talking about? We were freshmen; there wasn't much that we worried about. At this point in my life, my biggest fear was trying to get enough courage to talk to my crush, Brooke. She was beautiful, and every time I tried to speak to her, my knees went weak, and I started to stutter.

Besides that, I wasn't scared of much. In fact, our town was pretty boring. But finally I had the nerve to ask the question we were all thinking.

"If we don't have to worry about sinking, what do we need to worry about on the Cass River?" I asked.

"You boys do know Halloween is Saturday, right?"

"Dad, of course, we know that," David quickly answered. "We're too old for stupid trick-or-treating anyway. What does that have to do with our trip?"

We stood there holding our breath, waiting for Jim's answer.

"Just remember, it's a weird time to be on the

17

~ 5 ~

The legend of Scratchy has been told in our hometown for decades. The story has been used to scare kids every Halloween. Scratchy was a local celebrity in our town. I can remember at least three major nightmares after hearing the story for the first time as a fifth-grader.

Back in the late 1800s, the railroad system was booming across the country. It helped connect the east to the west and flooded the little towns with people along the way.

The railroad brought new trade and products to our town. It was an exciting time, with many families moving here and new opportunities arising.

James "Scratchy" Hatfield was one of the many men who worked on laying new tracks for the railroad expansion. His main job was using a heavy maul to drive home the spikes that held the rails in place.

Spike mauls are like sledgehammers, weighing between eight and twelve pounds. They're made of hardened steel and have a 12-inch head attached to them. One side of the maul is thinner and shorter. The longer side is used to spike over the tall railroad rails. The hickory handle was made for a comfortable grip, but it was known to get slippery in the rain, making it hard to control.

The job of a spike mauler was hard and meant long hours. Most maulers were stout and strong from swinging the weight of the large maul. It took a special kind of man to be on the spike mauler crew. Hatfield was one of those men.

All day and late into the night, Hatfield would pound and swing his large, heavy maul. He was strong and skilled, one of the best maulers on the railroad crew. Unfortunately for Hatfield, that would all change one rainy Halloween night.

In 1898, Hatfield was swinging his hammer late into the night when one of his apprentices needed help. Hatfield took his time, showing the young man the proper way to swing the large hammer without smashing into the rail. Feeling so confident in the man's ability, Hatfield bet the remaining men $3 that his apprentice could drive home a spike with one clean strike.

The other men took him up on the bet, and Hatfield volunteered to hold the spike. This was a violation of railroad policy and was very dangerous. Hatfield ignored the rule and thought it was a good way to show his apprentice that he had full confidence in his swinging ability. He also thought it would guarantee him success with the $3 bet.

The men gathered around with lanterns as Hatfield placed the spike and smiled at his apprentice. Rain was in Hatfield's eye, but he knew his apprentice was well trained to hit his mark.

The young apprentice was nervous that all eyes were on him and missed badly. Instead of hitting the spike, he hit Hatfield's wrist and hand. Folks there said they could hear Hatfield's scream from miles away.

Due to the impact and loss of blood, Hatfield passed out. When he woke up the next day, he was in a nearby hospital. Hatfield was groggy and struggled to see.

When his eyes finally focused, he looked at his hand. The hand was gone; nothing was there but a bandaged stub as a reminder of the dangerous bet he had lost. The doctors told him the hammer's force damaged his hand so much that they had no choice but to amputate it.

Unfortunately, Hatfield lost more than a hand that Halloween night.

Knowing his railroad days were now over, the sight of the bandaged stub was too much for Hatfield. That night as he laid in his bed, James Hatfield went crazy. The next day when the nurses came to check on him, he was gone. No one knew where or what happened to Hatfield. He was never seen or heard from again for the rest of the year.

Three years went by with no sign of James Hatfield. But on Halloween night in the fourth year of his disappearance, Hatfield made an appearance back on the railroad. A mysterious one-handed man was reported walking the tracks near the Lost Cemetery and Memorial Bridge. Several witnesses swear it was Hatfield.

The man was walking with his head down, and instead of two hands, the man had only one with a curved chrome shaped hook where the second should be. After seeing him, they heard an awful screeching sound in the distance that sounded like someone scratching metal together... or using a hook to scratch metal.

People were convinced that it was James Hatfield looking for his lost hand on the railroad tracks. From that day on and every Halloween since, locals claim to hear a loud scratching sound by the railroad tracks.

After that, other ghost stories have been told about a mysterious man with a hook haunting Memorial Bridge and the Lost Cemetery. Supposedly random scratch marks were found along the railroad tracks before the track was finally removed for good ten years earlier.

We were going to pass by both Memorial

~ 6 ~

A lump formed in my throat as I swallowed hard.

"Dad, stop!" David demanded. "Those old ghost stories aren't true, and you know it."

Jim just smiled. "I guess you'll see if they are or not."

I looked around. David, Johnny, and I were terrified, imagining Scratchy stalking us down the river. I turned to glance at Chris, but he, of course, just rolled his eyes. Chris didn't scare easily and definitely wasn't afraid of some old ghost story.

"I think we're going to catch some big fish," he said firmly. "I just want to fish. I plan on hooking into a big northern pike."

Okay, so the game was on. I couldn't look like a scared little baby. I straightened my stance and picked up my chin.

Jim changed the subject. "If you boys can make the trip without turning around and coming home, you'll have a chance to catch some River Kings!"

"River Kings?" I asked.

"Yep, River Kings are what we refer to when the giant, northern pike move out of their deep holes in the fall to hunt. A River King will be different than any fish you've ever caught. They're giants!"

Jim had our attention now. He added, "I've only caught a couple River Kings. I'll never forget the feeling of them on the end of my line."

Northern pike live in the Cass River but often have deep holes or hiding spots, making them hard to catch in the summer. During the fall, these big fish leave their safe place to fatten up before the long, upcoming winter.

"Yeah, I can dig that," Johnny said, relieved they had moved past the ghost story. "We need to catch some of those River Kings,"

We all nodded in agreement.

"If you boys can make it all the way to town,

you'll hook into one for sure," said Jim. He quickly added in a spooky, over-the-top voice, "*If you can make it.*"

What was David's dad trying to do? Did he think we would chicken out? We would be 14-year-old strong and athletic young men traveling down our local river. What's the worst that could happen?

It sounded easy, but I had no idea about the adventure and danger we would face as we rafted the Cass River.

Even the excitement of catching a River King couldn't get one thought out of my mind—*what's the worst that could happen?*

- 7 -

The rest of the week, we spent daydreaming about the fish we would catch and organizing supplies for our trip. School seemed to drag on even though it was only a three-day school week. By the time Wednesday hit, we were ready for school to be over so we could hit the river.

Kids get real goofy around Halloween. It might be because of all the candy and sugar or from the thrill of trick-or-treating. As freshmen, we felt that we were too old to do it—we had outgrown Halloween.

That didn't stop some kids from making the last day before break miserable. The Dowdy brothers, Ollie and Ryan, made a hobby out of terrorizing people around town. If you went to our school, you knew exactly who the Dowdy brothers were.

Some kids decided to dress up on Wednesday to celebrate an early Halloween since we wouldn't be in school again that week. Even though Halloween was on Saturday, the Dowdy brothers were going to use it as a bonus day to terrorize everyone at school.

Typical bullies, they came from a big family, with seven siblings spreading out in a bunch of grades at school. The youngest, Jimmy, was in first grade, and the oldest brother, Lance, was in twelfth grade.

The entire school was infected with Dowdys. I would like to tell you that they weren't all rude, horrible kids, but that would be a lie.

We were sure that every Dowdy woke up each day wondering how they could torment someone at school. Not only that, they usually all had failed a grade or two, making them way bigger than everyone in their class.

The Dowdy boys were big and strong. Every year we tried to convince them to play football because of their size and aggression, but they never played. We figured they didn't want to do anything to make other people happy. But if they would have played, they could have been unstoppable and helped us win more football games.

On Wednesday, everyone at school was loud. All the kids were excited about having a four-day weekend. The lunchroom was so noisy I could hardly hear the kids at our own table.

"I can't wait until tomorrow morning," David shouted at us.

"Me either. Let's leave tonight," Chris suggested with a big smile.

I quickly scanned David and Johnny's faces. I didn't want to admit it, but spending the night on the river without adults still scared me a little bit.

"Uh…we can't tonight," David yelled back.

Johnny and I nodded. We could have left then, but we were still a little scared of spending the night on the river. We needed one more day to gather our courage. Plus, we wanted to launch the raft in the morning, in the daylight.

According to plan, we were going to put the raft in around 10:00 Thursday morning and arrive at the pick-up spot at noon on Saturday.

We had convinced ourselves that if we launched during the day on Thursday, the two nights on the river would be easy. We were sure we had nothing to fear.

We were dead wrong!

~ 8 ~

"Sounds like fun! Can I go?" said a voice over my left shoulder. I turned to see Ollie Dowdy holding his lunch tray and standing directly behind me. Apparently, he had been eavesdropping and listened to our entire conversation.

We just sat there, stunned. I didn't know what to say. I didn't want to have the Dowdy boys after me today.

Finally, Chris spoke up. "There ain't enough room, now move along Ollie."

"Whatever, I don't want to go on your stupid trip anyway," Ollie said, swatting me on the back of the head. He left us and pushed two seventh-graders out of his way, clearing room for both him and his brother Ryan at the next table.

When Ryan sat down, I saw Ollie glaring in my direction and whispering to him with a devilish grin. I thought for sure they were planning on a food fight or jumping me in the lunchroom. But to my surprise, they looked away and starting picking on some other poor kid.

"That was close! Thanks again, Chris," I said and smiled.

Chris shrugged like it wasn't a big deal.

David returned to talking up our trip. "I cannot wait to get a line in the water tomorrow morning!"

"I got all kinds of snacks packed. My mom is making some caramel corn," I said.

If anything, I knew we would be eating great on the trip. Johnny's mom worked at the local grocery store, and she let us get a lot of snacks and junk food. A case of Tang, hot dogs, canned soups and ravioli, and bags of chips had lined our grocery cart.

"All the food is covered and the raft is ready. Are we missing anything?" Johnny asked.

"The fishing gear? Does everyone have their poles ready?" asked Chris.

Each of us had two of our best fishing poles

packed for the trip. I had added new fishing line since I didn't want my old line to break. I made sure I was ready to catch a River King.

"Everyone have at least three black and gold jointed Rapalas?" asked David.

A Rapala is a brand of fishing lure that resembles a small fish with two treble hooks attached underneath. The jointed lures were two separate pieces connected with a small screw. When the lure moved through the water, it swam just like a live minnow.

I made sure to have my lures ready. They were the first things I had put in my tackle box.

"My dad said the big ones, the River Kings, love a good black and gold Rapala in late October," explained David.

We went over everything one more time as we finished our school lunch. Chris read off the list and we all responded.

- "Food, heavy on the junk food"— "Check."
- "Fishing gear" —"Check."
- "Sleeping bags" —"Check."
- "Raft" —"Check."

Thinking about what Jim had said earlier, I wondered about courage. Courage? Maybe we weren't as prepared as I thought we were.

- 9 -

I slept well Wednesday night. I knew it was going to be the last time I was in my own bed for the next two nights.

While the big, pop-up tent would shelter us from the weather, I knew it wouldn't provide much warmth. I also knew that the raft was going to feel hard with only my lightly padded sleeping bag under me.

My mom dropped me off at David's at 9:00 a.m. sharp, the time we all had agreed upon. We had figured we would be able to put the raft in the water by 9:30.

That didn't happen. Johnny was late, and David didn't have any of his stuff ready. Chris and I sat on a nearby stump, talking and waiting for them to get their gear together.

Jim had taken the morning off work to help us

launch the raft. It was almost 10:30 by the time we had the raft loaded.

The atmosphere was light and full of excitement. What teenage boy wouldn't want to spend three days with his best friends fishing and camping? We were lucky our parents had agreed to let us go on the trip.

The four of us jumped onto the raft. Johnny and David had the oars, and Jim gave us a big push, pushing the raft off the sandy beach. We held our breath as the raft rocked and swayed, breaking away from the thick mud holding the barrels.

The raft floated perfectly! The river's current quickly straightened the raft, signaling the beginning of our adventure. I noticed the river was a lot higher and wider than usual. I had only been around the water during the summer, so I was shocked at how different it was during the fall.

I turned to say something to Chris and noticed he was already fishing. He was sitting on the right corner of the raft on a five-gallon bucket.

We were a competitive bunch; every one of us

wanted to be the one to catch the first River King. We all followed suit and soon had four poles in the water. It didn't take long before we started catching fish.

Another thing that shocked me about the river was the current. The current was moving fast, much faster than I had ever seen it. We had packed an old cement block and tied a big piece of rope to it for an anchor. We knew if we hit a good fishing hole, we could drop anchor and stop the raft.

We planned on trolling with our lines out most of the trip, especially the first day. We had to cover some serious ground to get to the first fishing hole in time so we would arrive at our pickup spot on schedule.

Jim figured it would take us all of two and a half days to float the river with minimal stops. He planned on meeting us at the downtown pick-up Saturday at noon.

We planned to anchor the raft at night and sleep in a fixed position. We didn't want to run into any trouble in the dark on the river. We also found comfort in being anchored in the middle of the river away from shore.

I turned and noticed David's house was already out of sight as the raft quickly turned the first bend in the river.

The scenery was gorgeous. Brilliant, bright colors decorated the fall leaves. The red hues varied from fire red to a dull light color with no two leaves the same. The yellow ones glowed almost as if they were sent directly from the sun. I took a deep breath and just enjoyed our surroundings. It was one of the most beautiful views I have ever seen.

The fishing started out good but wasn't great. We were catching some small rock bass and crappies. None of us had yet hooked into anything big like a pike, but this didn't surprise us. Jim had told us about three large holes along the way. They would give us our best chance at catching a giant River King.

The trip was off to a good start. The raft was working perfectly, and we were enjoying our fishing time.

The rhythm of the current hitting the rocks made a soothing sound as we floated peacefully down the Cass River. Suddenly I felt something nudge the raft, disrupting the currents' rhythm.

Chris felt it too and gave me an uneasy look.

We felt the bump again, but this time the raft came to a screeching halt. The force almost threw David overboard.

Peeking over the side into the pale blue water, I could make out a dark brown outline. It appeared that we had run into an underwater log jam. The heavy fall rains must have pushed some branches and trees into the river.

The force of the water was pushing on the back of the raft. The powerful current, combined with the raft's angle, started to pick up the back of the raft.

The raft was going to flip over on top of us!

~ 10 ~

The four of us ran to the back of the raft, using our weight to push it back down towards the water. Standing on the stern allowed the raft to steady itself but only temporarily.

"Someone is going to have get into the water to clear us off this jam!" David yelled, panicking. Typically, this would be a situation where Chris would just do what needed to be done and dive in. But Chris couldn't swim.

Johnny and I decided to do it together. We laid on our bellies, peering through the river water. Several logs had gotten stuck on a large rock, making a pinch point for them. The raft's weight caused the deck to dip deeper in the water, catching the top of the submerged logs.

We took off our shirts and sneakers and jumped off the edge of the raft. The force of our jump caused the raft to rock back and forth, which almost freed the raft from the logs.

The cold October water stung and numbed our bodies. The chilly shock startled me at first, but I quickly regained my composure and swam over to the side.

Johnny and I started rocking the raft back and forth as hard as we could. Chris and David helped by running from one side of the raft to the other as we shook it with our hands.

Slowly the raft started to move up towards the top of the log jam. We did this for a couple minutes and could see the raft getting closer and closer to being set free. Finally, we both gave it one big push, and the raft lurched forward, finally free. A huge sense of relief filled us all when the raft started floating down the river again.

"Grab this line and pull the raft towards the riverbank. We'll all get out and start a fire so you two can dry off," yelled David to us from the back of the raft.

Johnny took off, pulling the raft. I could see where David was anchoring up ahead.

I was tired of the cold water and decided to swim to the closest spot on shore. They were downriver about 25 yards from me, and I wanted to get out of the water as soon as I could.

As I got closer to the riverbank, I noticed a bunch of dead trees piled up. It looked like my only and best option to quickly get out of the river. The current was moving pretty rapidly, so I reached up and grabbed the biggest log I could find.

It took most of my strength to pull myself up onto the pile of trees. I collapsed on the pile, trying to catch my breath. The crisp air hit my cold, wet body, making everything feel heavy. My clothes suddenly felt like they weighed hundreds of pounds and clung to my body.

I was able to feel some relief by getting out of the current but knew I had to get warm fast. I took a deep breath and laid on my back for a couple seconds, thankful to be out of the frigid water.

I watched oak leaves float lazily across the sky. They were starting to hypnotizing me. All of a sudden, I felt a small tickle on my ankle. At first, I thought it was just a small branch poking through the rotting pile.

But one tickle led to many more, and I quickly sat up. I looked down towards my feet. My heart dropped; my entire left foot was covered in brown and gray snakes rolling and slithering around it.

I was laying smack dab in the middle of their nest!

~ 11 ~

I turned, looking down the river towards the guys, but they were too far away to help.

I tried to scream and couldn't—nothing came out! I knew I couldn't panic, but my heart was pounding so hard I thought it was going to break through my chest.

I made a split-second decision. I jumped up to my feet as fast as I could and dove back into the river. I felt a small, sharp sting as I surfaced.

Weird? I must have scratched my leg on a stick, I thought to myself. I swam down another 20 yards closer to my buddies to clear the snakes' nest.

I found a dry patch of the riverbank that extended into the water and crawled onto it. I instantly picked up my pant leg to see why it was burning. The first thing I saw was blood! As I looked closer and squeezed my leg, I saw two small holes. I had been bitten by one of the snakes when I jumped in the water!

"Dude, what happened?" David yelled over to me.

I turned to see my friends jogging down the bank to check on me.

"I just got bit by a snake!" I shouted back.

Chris and Johnny stopped to attend to me while David went to see the snakes' nest. Chris went back to the raft to get our emergency medical kit and returned with peroxide and a bandaid. The medicine stung when he poured it on.

"Guys, we have a problem!" yelled David.

Johnny helped me to my feet, and the three of us went down to see David and the snakes. When we got there, I could tell by David's face something was terribly wrong.

"Bobby, this is a rattlesnake den!" he cried out.

As soon as he said that, I started feeling sick, and the blood rushed to my head. I was about to pass out.

A rattlesnake den? Michigan has one very rare venomous snake called an Eastern Massasauga rattlesnake. Mr. Hill had talked about it when we did our science lessons on reptiles. But I remember him saying they are so rare he had never seen one in the wild.

They weren't as deadly as an Eastern diamondback but still were venomous and dangerous. I steadied myself on Chris' shoulder. I knew we were too far away from civilization to get help. My life started to flash before my eyes.

How could a fun trip turn into a deadly one? Even in my worst nightmare, I didn't think of a venomous snake taking my life on the Cass River.

Sweat was starting to bead up on the top of my head. I just knew I was minutes away from death.

"Aren't you supposed to suck the venom out or something?" I asked frantically of my friends as Chris crouched closer to the snakes to take a better look.

"I love ya brother, but I don't know about that," Johnny answered softly.

~ 12 ~

"I think you'll live," Chris said, laughing as he went back to the raft.

"Easy for you to say, you didn't get bitten by a rattlesnake," I shot back sharply.

"Yeah…and neither did you," he said. He stopped and turned to all of us.

"That isn't a rattlesnake—it's a water snake. They're found along rivers and streams. You can tell by the half-moon shapes on their belly. Don't worry, Bobby, they usually only eat minnows and frogs. I think you just woke them up before they had settled into their winter nap," Chris explained.

"Are you sure?" I asked, hoping he was right.

"One hundred percent positive. Now let's start that fire so you don't get something seriously dangerous like hyperthermia."

David quickly gathered branches and rocks and assembled a makeshift fire pit. Johnny and I jumped on the raft, grabbed some extra clothes, and sat by the fire to dry off. We hung up our wet clothes on a couple big tree branches overhanging us near the fire. The fall winds would work as a dryer for us if we needed more dry clothes later in the trip.

The fire and the fact that I wasn't going to die of a snakebite provided me with some big relief. David grabbed some hot dogs and cooked them for a much-needed snack.

We were only a couple hours into our trip and had already faced adversity. There was a sense of pride that we had managed to release the raft and survive a snake bite.

As we sat around the campfire, David told us a story about a big catfish he had caught when he was fishing with his brother. They had nicknamed the fish Big Lou.

The thought of fighting such a large fish excited all of us. After enjoying our snack, we threw dirt and water on the fire and put it out.

Then we loaded our stuff back on the raft. Johnny took his oar and shoved the raft off the low spot back into the river current. The snake bite had put us behind schedule; we needed to cover more ground before anchoring for the night.

The sun was starting to go down. I figured it was around 4:00 or 5:00 p.m.

Chris went and lit a small propane lantern we had brought. Besides flashlights, it would be our only source of light at night on the raft.

As it got darker, it was getting harder to cast without getting snagged on trees or rocks. I was about to put my pole down for the night when I figured I might as well make one more cast.

About halfway through reeling it in, I felt something big hit the lure and heard the reel's drag scream as the line was pulled.

Whatever it was, it caused my pole to bend and stretch. I could feel the fish on the other end. It was big, really big.

Did I just hook a River King?

~ 13 ~

The water made a lapping sound against the raft as David lowered the anchor. I tightened the grip on my pole as the big fish dove deep with the lure.

Johnny ran over with the net as Chris pulled in the remaining poles. We anchored about thirty feet from the hole where I had gotten the bite.

I battled the fish for a couple minutes, trying to let the fish run with the lure to wear itself out. Whenever I would pull or put force on the lure, I felt the fish fight back.

David grabbed the lantern and cast a glow on the water directly to the side of the raft. I bent over and brought the rod back up, forcing the fish to the top of the water. The fish broke the water and dove back down with one big swirl.

"That fish is huge!" Johnny cried.

I could feel it. I knew it was; there was no doubt it was a big northern pike, the kind that Mr. Hill told us about in science class. It was a River King!

As the fish dove, I decided to fight back with even more resistance. I reeled and pulled back harder than the time before. I could see the line getting closer and closer to the raft.

One more time, I reeled and rocked, bringing the rod up over my head. Suddenly, the tension on the line released, and I stumbled back, falling down on the raft. The line had broken; the big fish had won, and I had lost my first lure.

I had felt a River King on my line, and it felt amazing! I couldn't help wonder if I had just lost my only chance at getting a huge pike. Catching a River King was rare—did I just blow my chance?

I had battled a real, true River King, and it was everything I had imagined and more! The adrenaline rush was like nothing I had ever experienced.

"Dude, that was awesome!" David said softly.

"Yeah, man, we're going to get our hands on a

River King very soon," I said, determined to be the one to do so.

The four of us stayed and fished the hole where I had hooked the giant for another hour but with no more bites. River Kings were rare and smart; I knew he wasn't going to make the same mistake twice.

We all felt that hooking the fish was a good sign. It seemed like the weather and timing were perfect to hook a big fish on the Cass River. The big fish, the true River Kings, were feeding and looking to fatten up before the winter.

We floated and fished another couple of hours under the dark star-studded sky.

"Let's anchor here. It looks like a good spot to spend the night. We can fish more tomorrow," David suggested.

"Sounds good," said Johnny, ready for a break.

"Guys, just a heads up—we're a little behind schedule. We should have been another couple miles down the river by now," said Chris with a frown.

"No big deal, my dad knows we might be a couple hours late on Saturday. We can make up a little time tomorrow," said David.

"I'm not so worried about being late. Do you realize that means we're going to be crossing nearby the Lost Cemetery in the dark tomorrow night on Halloween?" Johnny asked with a shaky voice.

~ 14 ~

Yikes! When we mapped out our trip, we had planned on camping the second night about four miles past the cemetery. We were supposed to have left early on Thursday morning to avoid being anywhere near the Lost Cemetery in the dark.

"Why don't we stop a couple miles before the cemetery and camp tomorrow night?" Johnny suggested.

"We can't. We'll never make it to the pick-up spot on Saturday if we do that," Chris said with a worried look. "It would set us back almost a whole day. To keep to our timeframe, we'll have to float past the cemetery in the middle of the night."

"I don't think that's a good idea," David objected.

"Yeah, I agree with David," Johnny chimed in. "We don't want to be anywhere near the cemetery at night!"

"Time to grow up, boys, it's not an option. It's time for all of you guys to grow up," Chris declared. "Remember, everyone is already dead at the cemetery, and I'm not scared of any silly ghost story."

Chris wasn't, but the three of us were terrified of the cemetery and the legend of Scratchy. David's dad, Jim, hadn't helped the situation. If he hadn't brought it up, we might not even have thought of Scratchy's ghost story. But now that he had, I couldn't get it off my mind.

The adrenaline from fighting the fish vanished, and fear started to creep in. Tonight was the first night we were going to sleep alone on the river. When we were fishing, the excitement kept my mind busy. Now it was dark, and the river seemed spooky all of a sudden.

That night David rolled out a big metal burning barrel from inside the tent and built a fire in it. Johnny put a grate on top and cooked some beans and some smaller fish we had caught. The food tasted so good. We were all tired from the day's adventure, and dinner provided warmth and comfort.

Afterward, we stayed close to the fire and warmed our bodies for the long night ahead. Our plan was to sleep in the tent on the raft. While it would be cold, we had packed sleeping bags and blankets.

There was something magical in the dark, fall sky. There were no artificial lights to be seen anywhere—just the stars and the moon. Nature was all around us with no cars or people making noise. I had never seen the night sky look so beautiful. Scattered stars cast a glorious glow against the dark sky, and even the air seemed pure and flawless.

The four of us laughed and told stories; we started to feel like men—boys couldn't survive the river alone. After a couple of hours, we put out the fire and crawled into the tent.

At first, my sleeping bag was warm and inviting. The raft provided more comfort than I had anticipated, and I started to drift off to sleep.

Suddenly a loud, piercing howl broke the night's silence as it echoed down the river.

I had heard the noise before, but tonight it seemed a lot different. It was a coyote, but out here in the dark wilds of the river, it sounded much more terrifying.

I sat up and looked around the dark tent. Everyone else was asleep. I took my sleeping bag and moved it closer to Chris, just in case.

~ 15 ~

I didn't sleep well. Overnight temperatures dropped, and my sleeping bag got cold. Even though I didn't hear the coyote again, it was still hovering in the back of my mind throughout the night.

When Johnny shook me awake, it felt like I had just fallen asleep.

"Bobby, let's go—time to fish. You can sleep when we get home."

Chris and David were already fishing off the back of the raft. We caught some small crappie, just enough for breakfast, but no one hooked a River King.

David had the fire going once again and cooked the fish in some butter on his cast iron pan. The fish tasted good, and we vowed to have fish for breakfast the entire time during the trip.

"Guys, I was thinking last night. What if we don't fish as much and try to make up some ground today?" David asked.

"David, stop, man!" Chris shouted. "Grow up. We came on this trip to fish, to catch some big River Kings. Quit being a baby; we're fishing as planned."

And that was the end of the conversation. We all still felt the same way—all of us but Chris. I didn't want anything to do with the cemetery that night.

David pulled the anchor, and we were off for day #2 of our trip. The fishing was pretty good. We hooked a couple rock bass and some small largemouth bass. The river was the best part of the trip. It was like a highway for us, a way to explore. The fall colors continued to impress us and change along the river.

Around lunch, I saw a big 8-point buck drinking from the river. We floated by him in awe. His rack was high and white, and he had broad shoulders and a thick neck.

The buck held his head high like he was royalty in the woods. When we got closer, he bolted away, but it was amazing to have seen him so nearby.

We stopped and only anchored twice throughout the day. The first time was in a spot David felt was good. He said he had a magical feeling about it. We fished it for about an hour, but the only thing magical about it was how many snags we got.

Chris lost one of his prized lures and got mad. That was enough for us, so we pulled anchor and headed towards the second deep fishing hole.

David's dad, Jim, had drawn a makeshift map of the river. He had grown up fishing and trapping the river, so he was able to mark the good spots for fishing on it. We were about to hit the second spot, about a mile before the cemetery.

The sun was just starting to go down, and dusk was settling in when we arrived at the second hole.

"Are you sure you guys don't want to just keep going?" Johnny asked sheepishly.

Chris just shot him a look as he walked to the

back of the raft, dropping the anchor. There was no way around it—we were going to go by the cemetery in the dark!

- 16 -

We didn't want to look like wimps, but none of us really wanted to fish, except for Chris. We had wanted to get past the cemetery during daylight, but now it was too late. I watched as the rest of the sun disappeared, and the horizon turned black.

We fished the hole for another twenty minutes when Johnny hooked a big fish. He had learned something from me battling the big fish earlier. He fought the fish for over five minutes before its weight started to tire him out. Johnny was patient, but we were all anxious to see a River King up close.

He fought the fish for another ten minutes without making up much ground. The fish had taken about twenty yards of his line; Johnny only managed to gain about five yards back.

"Just be patient, we don't have anywhere to go

right now," Chris encouraged him.

Johnny held fast and kept pressure on the rod without reeling. He could feel the fish working the current and trying to gain leverage.

The drag on the rod squealed, and the fish tested him. The fish went to make another run, but Johnny countered. He could feel the fish tiring, so now he could reel and pump the rod to bring the fish to the side of the raft. Chris swooped down, netting the giant.

Of course, just like we all knew it would be, Johnny was the first one to catch a River King. The northern pike was really huge! David grabbed his tackle box to get his tape measure. The River King measured 38 inches!

Johnny sat back on his bucket, worn out. He flashed a big grin, knowing the satisfaction of catching a true River King. His face looked just like Mr. Hill's did on the slide in class—a look of appreciation and amazement.

During the fight, we all had gotten really loud and excited. Even though there were no houses around, we were sure you could have heard us a mile away. We were thrilled and didn't care if we were noisy. The rest of the world didn't exist; it was just the four of us alone on a Cass River adventure.

We had made an agreement before the trip. We were only keeping the fish we needed to eat; the rest we would catch and release. We were out of fish, so we decided to keep the big pike, and David filleted it for dinner. By the time we pulled anchor, it was well after 9:00 p.m. when I looked at my watch. It got dark earlier and felt much later than it was.

David hesitantly pulled the anchor, and the raft rocked back and forth before heading downriver. The four of us were quiet as we floated closer and closer to the Lost Cemetery.

The full moon slowly peeked out of the darkness, showing all its splendor. The moon was full and looked like a giant, white large pizza. We didn't even turn on the lantern because the moon provided all the light we needed.

"You guys realize that tonight at 12:01 a.m. it's Halloween?" asked Johnny.

Chris chuckled. David and I both smiled nervously.

"Look!" said David in awe.

There against the horizon in the distance was the eerie outline of the cemetery. The moon lit the banks of the river and illuminated the old wrought iron fence surrounding the cemetery. As we got closer, headstones materialized in the distance.

David took the lantern, went to the front of the raft, and announced, "Guys, we have a big problem." He pointed downriver.

One hundred yards in front of us, directly in the middle of the river, was a big fallen tree. Its trunk stretched from the left side of the river to the cemetery on the right size of the river where its top had landed.

David quickly dropped the raft's anchor.

We were now stranded in the middle of the river, next to the cemetery. Looking to our right, the background was full of headstones and statues.

It seemed like we had anchored the raft in the scariest spot possible.

"We can't make it through with that tree in the middle of the river," Johnny explained the obvious.

"We're going to have to figure this out in the daylight; it's too dangerous in the dark," Chris decided. "Looks like we're sleeping here tonight."

~ 17 ~

"Sleep here? Are you crazy?" I asked. If truth be told, I was as white as a sheet already.

"He's right, Bobby, we don't have a lot of options. We'll figure it out in the morning; we still have a lot of river to cover to make it to our pick-up," David agreed.

I looked back and noticed Chris and Johnny had already started fishing.

"What are you guys doing?" I asked.

"What do you want us to do? Hide in our sleeping bags? I came to fish!" Chris declared.

I didn't expect us to go to bed early or hide, but fishing was the last thing on my mind.

I couldn't take my eyes off the cemetery. I had never seen one at night; it was spooky. I squinted and could make out the old railroad tracks that ran directly parallel to the river next to the cemetery.

We were safe on the raft in the water, at least that's what I told myself. Unfortunately, that didn't add much comfort.

I went into the tent to grab my fishing pole when I heard excitement coming from David. Chris had something big hit his lure. Like a professional, Chris waited for the perfect time and set the hook. Chris had hooked a River King!

Maybe this place wasn't as creepy as I thought. It was a good thing the tree had fallen. There was no way we would have fished here otherwise. We had planned to get at least a mile past this point before anchoring for the night, but of course, the tree had changed our plans.

"He's a big one, boys," cried Chris as he muscled and fought the big fish. Judging by the arc in his pole, this fish looked bigger than David's.

"I got one too," Johnny yelled from the other side of the raft.

Two on at one time? The cemetery was producing some of the best fishing of the trip.

"You think you hooked a River King, Johnny?" I asked.

"I don't know. Whatever it is, it's heavy!"

David ran in and grabbed the lantern. I took a flashlight over to help Johnny.

Two River Kings at one time! Mr. Hill was never going to believe us. He told us we would be lucky if we caught two River Kings total, but we had two on at one time!

The nighttime air was filled with excitement and the loud hollering of the four of us.

"I hope we don't wake the dead," Chris said with a smirk.

"You're not funny, dude," I quickly shot back.

It took Chris another couple of minutes, but he finally pulled in his fish. It was a huge pike, bigger than David's. Chris had his River King! David grabbed the tape measure, and we were blown away that the fish measured 41 inches!

While we helped Chris land his fish, Johnny kept fighting his River King. For some reason, it seemed like he wasn't making much headway. The fish kept his weight on the line, but Johnny was only able to reel in a little piece.

Chris held his fish up in the moonlight; it's a

mental picture I'll never forget. He decided to let it go.

"I hope this fish can make someone else feel this good," he said. I was shocked; I had planned on eating fresh pike for dinner.

David brought the lantern over as we both encouraged Johnny.

"Guys, guys, stop," Chris said, coming over.

"What, I can't lose this fish!" Johnny grunted as he strained every muscle in his body to land the fish.

~ 18 ~

"Look!" Chris said, pointing out in the darkness towards Johnny's line.

I squinted as David swung the lantern towards where Chris was pointing.

"He doesn't have a fish; he has a snag," Chris explained.

Johnny's shoulders dropped, but the tension remained on the pole. In the distance, just outside the lantern's light, I could make out a big tree branch. Johnny had just fought for ten minutes with an oak branch that was in stuck in the river.

"Still felt cool for a while," Johnny admitted, trying not to sound sad.

We pulled in our fishing poles and went into the tent to eat dinner. We ate chips and cold hot dogs. They actually tasted pretty good but would have been a lot better if we cooked them over a campfire. David didn't even mention starting the fire. I was glad; I didn't want to draw any unwanted attention to our raft. I was sure you would be able to see the flames from the fire barrel from a long way away. I was okay with cold hot dogs.

I was also glad no one suggested going ashore. I didn't want to get any closer to the cemetery. After dinner, we played cards in the tent under the lantern light.

Without saying a word, Chris got up and crawled into his sleeping bag. Within minutes, he was snoring. Chris was a sound sleeper.

That left the three of us still awake. I had hoped to fall asleep before Chris, but I had gotten caught up in the card game and didn't realize Chris was tired. I was trying to be tough and not look like a wimp, but I could tell that both Johnny and David were just as scared as I was.

One by one, we crawled into our sleeping bags. I laid there, staring at the ceiling of the tent. I had convinced David to leave the lantern on for a couple minutes after we laid down.

"David, do you want me to shut the lantern off now?" I asked sheepishly, praying he would be okay if we left it on a little longer.

But he didn't respond. I sat up and looked over at them. David and Johnny were both already sleeping.

I was alone on Halloween night, just a hundred yards from the Lost Cemetery. I closed my eyes and tried to sleep, but my mind raced. This went on for a while before I finally started to feel my eyelids get heavy. I was just about to fall asleep when I heard a noise.

It was coming from the cemetery. It was loud and unmistakable. A long drawn out scraping sound came from the shore. The sound was high-pitched and reminded me of when someone runs their fingers across the chalkboard at school. The only problem was, there was no chalkboard, and we weren't anywhere near the school.

I knew what the sound was; I knew right away. It was Scratchy! He was out on Halloween, searching the cemetery for a new hand.

After a couple minutes of silence, I heard the

- 19 -

I tried to wake up Johnny, but he just mumbled something and rolled over. I tiptoed to the front of the tent and slowly unzipped the front. I peeked towards the cemetery. The backdrop was like something out of a spooky horror movie.

The moonlight cast an eerie white shadow over all the graves. Even though it was dark, the full moon made it easy to see.

The autumn wind was blowing, just enough to make everything along the riverbank come to life. Branches danced and swayed like scarecrows guarding a farmer's field.

My face was exposed to the fall breeze, and I could taste fall on my tongue. I stared towards the cemetery and was spooked every couple of seconds by a nearby branch moving in the wind.

"There's nothing out there," I heard a voice

behind me say. I jumped, startled since I didn't think anyone else was up. I was relieved to see Chris. He was the one I would pick to be up with me.

"I heard a noise. Something's not right," I said. Chris came over and swung open the front of the tent. He stood there, staring out in the night sky and stretched.

"I don't see anything," he said.

"Well, I didn't see anything either. I *heard* it," I insisted.

"Probably just another coyote," he replied.

I knew it wasn't a coyote...I knew exactly what it was.

Chris pushed his way back through the opening of the tent and turned to zip it up.

"Bobby, go to bed. You're going to need some sleep. We have a busy day tomorrow," Chris told me.

I went back into the tent and crawled into my sleeping bag. Within seconds of zipping up my bag, the quiet, calm night was once again broken by the scratching sound. This time, Chris heard it and sat up. It was the first time I had ever seen a look of concern on Chris' face. The sound was so close, this time I made sure to wake up David and Johnny.

"That is *not* a coyote!" Chris whispered.

"Definitely not a coyote," I whispered back.

David wiped his eyes and got up to turn on the lantern. Chris grabbed his arm to stop him.

"We don't need that tonight," he said firmly.

David looked confused but knew now wasn't the time to argue with Chris. The four of us followed single file behind Chris as he quietly unzipped the tent.

We walked out to the edge of the raft. I could not imagine a scarier situation than the one we were in. As we stood there, I noticed my body was trembling. I tried to convince myself that I was just cold, but I knew that was a lie. I was terrified.

I glanced over at Johnny and watched as he slowly pulled both of his hands back into his coat. He was thinking the exact same thing.

Scratchy had returned on Halloween looking

for a hand. What happened if he didn't find one in the cemetery?

Was the raft the next place he planned on looking?

~ 20 ~

"Maybe we should jump in the river and head to the opposite shore," David suggested.

The other shoreline was too steep and rocky to get up on. That meant there was only one direction we could go—straight towards the cemetery.

"Don't tell me you want us to head towards the cemetery, towards Scratchy?" whispered Johnny.

"Scratchy, come on, man. You don't actually believe that tale. We're too old for that, Johnny!" Chris whispered back.

I chimed in. "Then what, Chris? You explain to me what the noise is then. You know it's no coyote," I insisted.

"Could be a million things, I can guarantee it's not an old made up ghost story about some lunatic looking for his lost hand," he said firmly.

Thinking about the story, it didn't make sense. I was old enough and smart enough to know that ghost stories weren't true. Still, there was something about the old railroad tracks and cemetery that made it seem believable.

"Did you see that?" whispered David.

The rest of us squinted towards the side of the cemetery where David was pointing. Behind one of the headstones appeared to be the outline of a person. It was hard to make out who it was, but it looked like someone was staring right at us.

"Let's head back into the tent," Chris said softly. It was the first time in my life I ever heard a little doubt in his strong voice.

That was all we needed to hear. We sprinted into the tent, and I dove into my sleeping bag. We were all in such a hurry that no one zipped up the entrance to the tent. The wind caught the tent flaps, and they were flailing in the wind and making an awful sound.

"You better go shut it, Johnny," I said. He was the fastest, so naturally, he was my first choice.

"I'm not getting up," Johnny declared.

I looked around. The four of us were in the far corner of the tent, and no one really was too anxious to get up and zip up the tent.

I mustered up every ounce of courage I had and hurried towards the opening. I reached up, but just before zipping it up, I gave one quick glance out towards the headstone where the mystery figure stood.

Whatever it was, it was gone. But there was no doubt about it—someone had been there in the cemetery.

"What do you see, Bobby?" asked Chris.

I turned. "That's the problem, I don't see anything now."

They all knew what that meant. Someone or something was after us.

We were all shaken by the strange noises and the mysterious figure we saw in the graveyard. We curled up near each other in the back of the tent.

This time, I made sure I wasn't the last one to fall asleep. I could hear Johnny and David arguing about the legend of Scratchy. For some strange reason, I found a sliver of comfort hearing them debate with each other. I knew as long as they kept talking, that meant they were awake. I wanted to use this to my advantage. I was determined to not be the last one awake again.

My eyelids got so heavy I couldn't keep them open. They would have to fend off Scratchy without me.

~ 21 ~

Sometime in the middle of the night, something woke me. It wasn't the loud scratching noise from earlier in the night. This noise was different, quieter and definitely much closer. I scanned the tent and made out the outline of my sleeping friends. The moon shone through several holes in the roof, providing just enough light to see. There was also a faint outline where the zipper ran.

Other than that, the tent was dark. I didn't know what time it was, but I knew I had been sleeping for a couple of hours at least.

I laid motionless, staring at the front of the tent and trying to figure out what I was hearing. I wanted to move, to spring into action and protect my best friends.

For some strange reason, I couldn't move. I

was frozen. It was like my entire body was stuck in cement. The only part of my body I could move were my eyes, and they stayed fixated on the zipper of our tent.

Slowly, the zipper's pull started to move up from the bottom. Larger beams of moonlight starting showing as the zipper was coming up.

Someone was unzipping our tent!

Still paralyzed, I tried to say something—yell to scare the person away or wake up my friends—but I couldn't. I was completely helpless, staring as the front flap to the tent was fully unzipped.

Standing in the outline of the moon was a man. He was old and pale with creases all over his face. His white hair was long and the same color as the moonlight. His clothes were strange. I could tell right away they were from a different moment in time.

My eyes scanned their way down his body and focused on his hands. Or should I say hand...

On his left arm, there was a hand; but on his right hand, was a silvery, chrome hook. The man took two steps into the tent.

The front flap closed behind him, making the tent dark again. Now without the moonlight, I could only make out his dark silhouette inching closer towards me.

He walked slowly, methodically, towards the cluster of us at the back of the tent. I watched as he bent down. The odor of death filled the tent.

I watched in horror as he reached back with his hook and lunged into my arm!

- 22 -

The pain in my arm was excruciating! It startled me, and suddenly, my body was alert. I was able to move again! I quickly rolled over and tried to get free from the sharp hook on my arm.

The pain in my arm intensified, and my vision started to go dark. I couldn't escape Scratchy. He had been after me all night, and now he had his hook into me. There was nothing else I could do. There was nothing anyone could do. He had me; there was no escape.

"Bobby, Bobby, wake up, man," I heard a voice calling. I opened my eyes to see Chris standing over me, tugging on my arm.

"I think you had some kind of bad dream or something," he explained.

Wet with sweat, I quickly sat up. As my vision became clear, I noticed it was morning, and I had survived the night. It had been all a horrible dream. My imagination had gotten the best of me. The constant talk of Scratchy and the night's events produced one of the worst nightmares of my life.

Chris walked back out, leaving me alone in the tent.

"Bobby, get out here!" David yelled.

I made it outside to find all three of them at the back of the raft, looking towards the cemetery.

Above us on the river bank, a big oak tree was shedding its leaves. They floated all around us, landing on the raft and in the river. I moved closer to David as they were all staring towards the cemetery. Chris pointed to a huge elm tree that bordered the railroad tracks directly off the shore about ten yards away from the cemetery entrance.

There freshly scratched into the tree was my name. It was as clear as the fall sky, carved in big capital letters—BOBBIE.

I just stared in disbelief.

There was no way that was there last night. The bark was still a light brown and hanging from each letter. It was apparent this had been carved in the last couple of hours.

Finally, I broke the awkward silence. "Okay, Chris, explain that," I demanded.

"That's weird, I will admit," Chris replied. "But I wouldn't get too worried. They didn't even spell your name right," he pointed out.

He was right. Whoever it was had misspelled my name.

"We are out in the middle of nowhere. We heard crazy weird noises, and now my name is etched into a tree ," I said, shaking my head.

"Whoever it was, it didn't get you, so that's good," said Johnny.

"Yeah, right. That makes me feel so much better."

"We got bigger problems," David said. "Someone is going to have to get wet again. We have to get this tree out of our way so we can get out of here! We're way behind schedule and have to meet my dad in four hours."

"And we still have two River Kings to catch," Chris reminded us.

I was relieved that was our last night to sleep on the river. There was a part of me that was proud we had survived two nights alone on the river. It seemed we weren't alone, but there was comfort in knowing I would be in my own bed tonight.

David and I were the only ones still without a River King, but that seemed like an afterthought now. I just wanted to get home alive.

Johnny, David, and I jumped into the frigid river and swam over to free the log. Chris rolled out the burning barrel and started a fire to dry off when we got back. As I swam in the cold water, I was thankful David had decided to bring the barrel with us. It had provided good heat for cooking and for drying off.

As we approached the fallen tree, I was surprised at how big and healthy it was. It wasn't dead and looked to have a lot of years left. For some reason, it was down, blocking our escape.

The weight of the tree was more than we thought it would be. It took all three of us to move it. We pushed and swam with it towards the opposite rocky shore.

"Let's get it on shore just enough so the end of the tree is out of our way. Then we can continue down the river," David suggested.

Johnny and I jumped up on the edge of the river onto a big rock while Chris walked on the top of the tree towards us. The three of us rolled the tree back towards the other side.

"Hey, come here. Look at this!" Johnny cried.

I walked over to the trunk. There at the base of the trunk were saw marks.

"Dude, this tree didn't fall down. Somebody cut it down," I said to Johnny. "For sure, no doubt about it. They had to have done it yesterday."

"Why would anyone want to cut this tree down?" Johnny asked.

"So we would have to stop here for the night," I explained.

By now, the three of us were freaking out. David crawled onto the shore and looked at it. He agreed; someone had deliberately cut this tree down to stop us from going down the river. Someone wanted us to be in front of the cemetery last night.

I was convinced that Scratchy wouldn't stop until he got one of us...or one of our hands. For some reason, I seemed to be the one he was after.

But why me?

~ 23 ~

The three of us swam back to the raft. David soon had the fire roaring, and we changed out of our wet clothes. Then we huddled around the burning barrel as the raft floated down the river once more.

"Guys, I'm afraid that we aren't going to be able to stop and fish anymore," David explained. "If we go straight through, we're still going to be a couple hours late to our rendezvous point in town."

I listened but kept both eyes on the river bank. I continually scanned the underbrush and tree lines. I hoped that Scratchy's shiny, chrome hook would reflect in the autumn sun.

"Bobby, if he really wanted you, he would have grabbed you last night," Chris said.

"Maybe he can't swim," Johnny suggested.

"You guys are really funny, but your name wasn't carved into that tree," I said.

"Even so, you need to stop worrying and start fishing," said Chris.

David and I were the only two left that hadn't been able to slay a River King. I was thankful my friends wanted us to catch one.

At least David had a snag, something to get him a little excited. Me, I hadn't caught anything big the past two days. David and I went to the back of the raft and starting casting while the raft traveled down the river. But I still kept my eyes alert for any sign of Scratchy.

Two hours into the morning trip, David felt a fish hammer his lure. He set the hook, and the fight was on. I could tell right away that he had finally hooked a River King. I was happy for David but nervous at the same time. Would I be the only one who didn't catch a River King?

The fish went on multiple runs, but David had set the hook perfectly. In the end, David won and hauled in a beautiful northern pike, another true River King. His fish was a big female and measured 42 inches, one inch bigger than Chris' fish. The belly on the female hung low, and the fish was also the heaviest one of the trip.

The trip had already been eventful, filled with highs and lows. To be honest, I really did want to feel the power and strength of a River King. After watching David, I knew the trip wouldn't be complete for me unless I hooked a River King.

Ever since that day in Mr. Hill's science class, I felt the next step in becoming a man was to catch a River King. My three best friends had, but as the morning went on, it didn't look good for me. We had already fished two out of the three known pike spots. It didn't seem like we would have enough time to fish the third and final hole. The best fishing was behind us, and it had produced well, just not for me.

The river fishing adventure had been incredible in so many ways. To spend three days fishing and camping on a raft with your three best friends is something few people ever get to do.

We had survived a scary night at the cemetery. Even though it was still a mystery, nothing terrible had happened to us; we were all still alive and whole, but the mystery of who was after us was still confusing.

I had so many questions. Who cut the tree down to block our way down the river? Why was my name carved out on a tree near the cemetery? As I sat there thinking, I decided maybe it was better if I didn't know the answer to my questions.

I decided to try to fish as hard as I could until we got to the pick-up area. I was casting and reeling furiously, trying to get my lure in the water as many times as possible until our trip ended.

I looked at my watch, it was 11:00 a.m., and we still had quite some ways to go before meeting David's dad.

"Hey guys, there's the Memorial Bridge," yelled David.

I turned to see the old railroad bridge arching over the top of the Cass River. The bridge looked much bigger than I had thought; I had only seen it in pictures. I knew that Memorial Bridge was built during the railroad days of our town. Now, rust and graffiti littered the once beautiful bridge. We were all staring when Chris started hollering my name.

"Bobby, come on, man! Come to the back of the raft, let's fish," Chris said quickly. It surprised me that he sounded so anxious. Why did Chris care if I looked at the bridge? For some reason, he was trying to distract me.

I turned away from him and glanced back towards the old bridge just as we were about to pass under it. The shadow of the bridge cast a dark shadow over the raft.

Then I saw it… Spray painted in big, bold red letters was my name—BOBBIE!

- 24 -

Any doubt that someone wasn't pursuing me disappeared when I saw the writing on the side of the bridge. I knew what we all knew—someone was definitely after me.

Memorial Bridge was around three hours by raft from the downtown pick-up where Jim would be waiting for us.

"Everything will be fine. We just need to get to the pick-up," Chris said.

"My dad is going to be really worried; he told me to make sure we weren't late," David said, frowning.

"Nothing we can do about it now. He'll be fine once he hears about our trip and the River Kings we caught." Chris was being practical again.

"You're probably right," agreed David.

"What about…" I began.

"Don't bring it up, Bobby, we'll take care of each other. We're safe as long as we stay in the river. I don't think Scratchy can swim," Chris noted.

I walked back to the rear of the raft and continued to fish. I noticed that Chris and David were no longer fishing. Now they were watching.

I could tell they were concerned because too many things were off. This was no coincidence. Something was wrong.

One hour went by, and nothing happened. Then another and still nothing, just a raft full of kids passed us, furiously paddling down the river towards downtown.

The current pushed the raft at a good pace down the river. I glanced at my watch. It was noon, and we still were a couple miles downriver of town. At best, we were going to be at least two hours late.

"Good news, boys. Look, in the distance," David said, pointing to the shore.

There was an old, weathered building that

used to be the Great Lakes Railroad Station. The roof had collapsed, and all the windows were smashed out of it. Two of the walls had collapsed, leaving an odd-shaped structure.

"You got to be kidding me," I shouted as we floated by the building.

There, on one of the only standing walls was more red spray paint. Someone had written BOB with the next B started but not finished.

"Someone was just writing this and stopped in the middle of spray painting your name on the wall," said David.

"That means whoever it is, they're close. And they know where we are and where we're going," Chris said softly.

"The good news—we're only about a mile from town and the pick-up," said Johnny.

I took a long, drawn out deep breath. We could make it a mile. Even though everything looked the same on the river, I knew downtown wasn't far away.

As I went to cast my pole, I felt something solid bump the bottom of the boat. It was subtle at first, but the next thing I knew, there was a loud boom! I watched as two of the barrels ripped from the raft and start floating downstream.

We grabbed whatever we could get our hands on before jumping off the side of the raft. In a matter of seconds, two pieces of the raft were torn apart, and some of the debris began floating down the river.

The river's current caught me, tossing my body around the chilly river. I grabbed a nearby log, stopping myself from being taken down the river.

What about Chris? I thought. *He can't swim...*

- 25 -

I crawled ashore, cold and shaken. The river's water was frigid, and the sudden sinking of the raft was a shock. Before I jumped off, I managed to grab my backpack.

I stood up and looked down the river. There were pieces of wood and debris floating everywhere. Twenty yards down the riverbank, I saw David pulling himself up out of the water. I scanned the other bank and saw Johnny lying on the river's edge just across from me.

Where was Chris?

"Guys! Chris? Where's Chris?" I yelled, now sprinting down the riverbank towards David. David was getting his bearings back as I approached.

"I don't know, I didn't see him jump," David shouted.

"He can't swim!" I yelled back.

I started sprinting down the bank of the river and yelling Chris' name. I scanned the water as I ran by, looking for any sign of Chris. There was debris, clothing, and wood from our raft all over the river.

About 100 yards past David, something caught my eye—a big chunk of the raft had gotten tangled up in some branches in the river. The branch caught the raft and held it from being swept away by the current.

I squinted and saw something sitting on the raft. As I got closer, I could tell it was a fishing pole. I walked the big oak branch down and reached to grab the pole.

It was Chris' pole, and thankfully, I saw his hand firmly attached to it.

"About time you got here!" Chris said. His other hand was tightly grasping the large chunk of wood that had saved him from the river.

I crawled onto the wood and pulled him out of the river. David and Johnny joined and helped by wading in and freeing up the jam. Chris was finally out of the water, and the four of us were safe. The temperature had been dropping all day, and it was getting colder by the minute. We knew hyperthermia was more dangerous than drowning now. Luckily, I had some waterproof matches in my backpack and quickly started a fire on the river bank.

We sat around the fire, broken but not beaten. Our raft was not going to be able to take us down the river anymore. We had less than a mile walk to safety.

Suddenly, Chris started laughing.

"What a rush, boys! We conquered this river!" he cried out.

The burst of confidence was what we all needed. We started giving each other hugs and high fives. I had survived a snake bite, a ship-wreck, and a ghost.

But we weren't home yet…

~ 26 ~

After warming up and drying off, we started the trek down the riverbank towards our pick-up spot. It was uncomfortable walking. Even though we had dried off, our clothes were stiff and made us feel clumsy.

The river's edge was rocky and coarse, making the mile walk much harder. After about ten minutes, Chris stopped and turned to me.

"Bobby, we're already late, so get this pole in the water," he said, handing me the pole he had worked so hard to save.

Fishing? That was the last thing on my mind. I was ready to be home safe.

"Nah, Chris, I'm good. I just want to get home."

"Hey man, that's up to you, but I know I wouldn't want to be the only one that didn't hook a River King. I mean isn't that a big reason why we came?" he asked me with a smile.

It was, but by now, I was just hoping to make it home alive.

"I'm good, man," I replied.

"Okay," he said.

We walked for another couple of minutes and came to an opening in the river that widened by at least 30 feet before narrowing back to its normal size. It was the last hole that David's dad Jim had told us about. This was the same hole where he had caught his River King.

"You've got to fish this spot; it's the last one," Johnny urged me. "We're almost back to the pick-up, and we're already late."

I was hesitant, but part of me really wanted to feel a River King on the end of my line.

"Dude, my dad is already going to be freaking out," David argued.

"David, how about lets you and me finish walking to the pick-up point so your dad knows we're safe," Chris suggested. "Let Bobby try one more time to catch one. He'll be right behind us."

"I'll stay back with him," Johnny offered.

Chris handed me the last pole, the only one that survived the trip. Thankfully there was still one black and gold Rapala on the other end.

"We'll wait for you downriver at the pick-up spot. Fish this hole for about twenty minutes; then you follow the river. We'll be waiting," said David.

With that, Chris and David took off to meet Jim at the pickup point. I could hear cars in the background and knew we were close to town.

I looked at my watch—it was 2:40. I did just as Chris said and fished for 20 minutes. I didn't get a single bite, nothing.

"There aren't any fish here. Let's go," I decided.

Johnny was in agreement, and we took off.

After a couple hundred yards, we could make out the faint sounds of police sirens. Something was wrong, terribly wrong.

~ 27 ~

We picked up our pace and started jogging towards the sirens. After a couple of minutes, we turned and rounded the last bend in the river before we hit the pick-up spot.

In the distance, we could see police lights and hear sirens coming from near our pick-up point. There were a bunch of cars there along with at least two police cruisers. People were everywhere. Panic sat in as Johnny and I started sprinting towards the noise.

Did something happen to David and Chris?

The loose rocks on the riverbank made running difficult. Without any warning, my left boot lost its footing, sending me crashing to the ground. Chris' fishing pole went flying into the water, and I landed hard on some really jagged rocks.

"Are you okay, Bobby?"

"Yeah, I'm fine, just a little bruised. I think I twisted my left ankle, but I'm good."

Johnny helped me up. I made sure to wade into the water to retrieve Chris' pole. The pole was important to all of us now—it had survived the trip with us. There was no way I was going to leave it behind. It was all we had left.

Luckily the pole wasn't broken. With Johnny at my side, I started limping towards the commotion. We were close, probably only a hundred yards away from everyone.

We were in a hurry to see what the noise was all about. I hadn't noticed that the lure had come off my pole and was loose in the water.

As we got closer, a woman pushed her way through the crowd. It was Johnny's mom; she sprinted up and bear-hugged Johnny. All of our parents were there, plus about 50 or more friends, family, and community members.

"I thought you were dead!" she cried, gripping Johnny as hard as she could.

"Mom, we're fine. We're only a couple hours

late, Mom," said Johnny, embarrassed his mom was making such a big deal.

Johnny's mom went on to tell us that somebody was fishing on the dock near our pick-up site when a tent and a bunch of kids' clothes floated by on the river. He went to the police station and told Sheriff Mike, who happened to be Johnny's dad.

The sheriff knew we were on the river and recognized some of the clothes. He called home, and within minutes, Johnny's mother organized a community search party.

The sirens and craziness were all for us. Even the local newspaper was there taking pictures, proving that not much happens in our small town.

We walked over and saw Chris and David sitting wrapped up in blankets on the back of Jim's truck, which was parked just off the river.

"Hey, boys, who would have thought we were so important?" David said with a big smile. "What a mighty adventure we had down the Cass River!"

"Oh good, you still got my pole," said Chris,

pointing to my right hand. I had almost forgotten that I still carried it.

"Looks like the line came off. Better reel it in before it gets snagged," said Chris. I took a couple steps back towards the river and started reeling it in. But it was too late—the line was already snagged on something.

"Man, I hope I don't have to walk all the way back down to where I fell," I said to Johnny, who was still standing near the tailgate of the truck.

"Just break the line," he said.

"Don't the break the line! That's my last lure!" cried Chris.

He was nice enough to let me use it, so I had no intentions of breaking the line. I figured it had gotten caught on some rocks where I had fallen, which was about seventy yards back down the river.

I started to leave the crowd and walk back down the river towards the snag. I was about fifty yards down when I stopped to recheck the line.

I reached back and gave it a half-hearted jerk on the pole to see if I could free the lure without having to limp all the way back down the river.

When I jerked, the line came to life and took off down the river. It wasn't a snag—it was a fish!

~ 28 ~

The line roared off the reel, making a loud screeching sound.

"Hey, Bobby, you got a fish!" David yelled from the tailgate.

I turned.

"I think so; I think it's pretty big too!"

The guys jumped off the tailgate and ran towards me. Others in the crowd noticed my rod bending and the reel squawking loudly. Before I knew it, I was surrounded by excited onlookers.

Fighting the fish was both exhilarating and exhausting all at the same time. It was hard to put weight on the line with my bum left ankle. The fish put together several runs; each time, I put more weight on the line and reeled in what I could.

I was losing ground on the fish. It was taking

my line further and further back down the river.

"Just keep it on him; the current will help you fight this fish," Jim yelled out to me.

He was right. The current was working in my favor as the fish tried to race directly against it. He was fighting me and the rapid river current at the same time. The fish gave me one last furious run, which I countered by backing up and reeling as hard as I could.

The weight of the fish shifted, and I could feel it getting closer. There was one more attempted run, which I countered with more pressure and reeling.

"There he is!" shouted Johnny, pointing into the river. The fish was visible, making it easy to see its reddish fin, olive skin, and clear white belly.

"Grab the net!" I yelled.

"Bobby, we don't have the net. It's at the bottom of the river somewhere," David reminded me.

"Just don't overdo it with the fish; let him wear himself out," Chris directed me.

And that's exactly what I did. I planted my right foot and leaned back on the pole. I used my body weight to fight the remaining power of the fish.

Two minutes later, I started reeling it in, slowly bringing the fish closer to shore. The big pike was tired and seemed ready to give up the fight. I started reeling and pumping on the rod, bringing the fish the remainder of the way to shore.

Suddenly there was a huge splash. Chris had jumped into the water and secured the fish. When he brought him out of the water, I couldn't believe it—I had caught a true River King!

The crowd went crazy, cheering loudly. Chris walked up the bank of the river and handed me my fish. He was big, bigger than all the others we had caught on our trip. A newspaper reporter ran over, and the four of us posed holding the giant northern pike. When we measured it, the fish was 45 inches long.

Holding the monster pike made me feel like a rock star. Later that week, the newspaper printed our picture on the front page.

The four of us survived a crazy adventure, and each caught a River King. It was one of the best days of my life. We were the true River Kings that fall!

And Hugh, that's the end of my story about the River King.

~ 29 ~

"Wait one second, Grandpa. What do you mean the end?" asked Hugh. The quick ending surprised him, and he had a lot more questions for his grandpa.

"That's the end. That's when I learned that every second your line is in the water is important. That event changed my life forever. Just because you don't catch something on the first cast, doesn't mean you give up. Sometimes it only takes one more cast," Grandpa said.

"Come on, are you kidding me? You have to finish the story," Hugh pleaded.

Grandpa then told Hugh that the four guys stayed in touch, and he was still close with two of them. David went on to be a successful electrical engineer and ran a million-dollar company just outside Detroit. Every year, he and Bobby spent a week together at a deer hunting camp in the Upper Peninsula of Michigan.

Johnny became an all-state athlete in football, basketball, and baseball. He had a small stint in minor league baseball but ended up throwing out his arm, which ended his career. He and Bobby were still close and talked almost every day. After high school, Johnny moved to a small college in Florida and worked as a professional baseball scout for the Detroit Tigers. Bobby spends the month of January down in Orlando with Johnny. They do a lot of deep-sea fishing in the ocean.

"What about Chris? What happened to Chris?" Hugh asked.

"Well, Chris, he gave the ultimate sacrifice. We lost Chris in the Vietnam War. Chris joined the Army and was in Special Forces. He went on to become a war hero and saved many lives in the military. He was awarded one of the highest awards in all of the military, the Purple Heart. It's the oldest military award still given to U.S. military members. Hugh, have you ever noticed the sign displayed when entering our town. It has

Chris' name on it, honoring his heroism and sac-rifices. Chris sacrificed himself to save other sol-diers."

But the story still wasn't over, and Hugh started to squirm in his chair. There was one big part of the story that Grandpa hadn't told yet.

"Grandpa, whatever happened to Scratchy? Did he ever find you or bother you again? Did you ever figure out why he was after you?"

Grandpa started laughing.

"I got my answer two weeks after our fishing trip. I was sitting in Mr. Jones' math class when the teacher paired us up in groups of two to work on a math sheet. He partnered me with Ollie Dowdy," Grandpa explained and began laughing again.

Grandpa was finally able to get it together and finish the story, "We had to first put our names on the paper. Ollie had the pencil so he wrote his name, then I told him to write mine. When he did, he spelled it B-O-B-B-I-E at the top of the paper. That's when I solved the mystery of old Scratchy!"

About the Author

Lane Walker is an award-winning author, speaker, and educator. His book collection, *Hometown Hunters*, won a Bronze Medal at the Moonbeam Awards for Best Kids Series. In the fall of 2020, Lane launched another series called *The Fishing Chronicles*.

Lane is an accomplished outdoor writer in the state of Michigan. He has been writing for the past 20 years and has over 250 articles professionally published. Walker has a real passion for outdoor recruitment and getting kids excited about reading. He is a former fifth-grade teacher and elementary school principal. Walker is currently a director/principal at a technical center in Michigan.

Walker is married with four amazing children. Find out more about the author at www.lanewalker.com